Special Gifts

In Search of Love and Honor

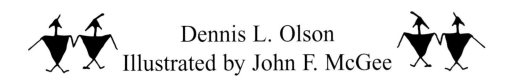

Dennis L. Olson
Illustrated by John F. McGee

NorthWord Press
Minnetonka, Minnesota

Long, long ago,
after Creator had made the World,
he made two very special things.
He called them "Love" and "Honor."
They were his Special Gifts to the World.

4

Love helped parents feel good about each other, and about their young. Love helped neighbors get along and be kind to each other.

Honor helped them all be truthful and trust each other. It helped them learn from their mistakes. Honor helped them do their *best*—whatever they tried.

But Creator had one worry. It was the Two-leggeds. A few of them might become confused and twist Love and Honor for selfish reasons. They might make things *seem* like Love and Honor when they really weren't. So he asked the animals for help to protect the Special Gifts.

6

Early in the morning, Eagle came soaring from the East. Eagle was the keeper of the dawn, and the messenger from the sky. He offered to fly the Special Gifts far up into the sky—even to the Moon. "That will be a good hiding place," he told Creator.

8

Creator thought about Eagle's offer for a while, then shook his head.

"They will find them there," he said. "One day, another flying thing will land on the Moon. It will have Two-leggeds inside, and they will find the Special Gifts."

About noon, Mouse scurried to Creator from his home in the South. Mouse was the keeper of the warm, green summer. He offered to take the Special Gifts and bury them under the miles and miles of grass on the prairie. "That will confuse them. The prairie is so big."

Creator thought this idea might work, and then he shook his head.

"No," he said. "Those Two-leggeds will someday turn over the whole prairie with their iron plows. They will think it *all* belongs to them. They will leave no room for the First People or the Buffalo. And they will find the Special Gifts."

At sunset, Bear lurched to where Creator sat, huffing his way from his home in the West. Bear always stayed near the sunset because he was the keeper of the night. He offered to take the Special Gifts to the high mountains and dig a deep cave. "If I put them there, the rocks will be too heavy for the Two-leggeds to dig, and they will give up."

Creator thought, and then shook his head again.

"Those Two-leggeds are clever," he said. "One day they
will take giant machines and dig the rock away. They will
be looking for shiny things. They will find the Special Gifts
because they will dig holes in the Earth as big as the
mountains."

When it was dark, the night cooled the air, and Wolf loped to where Creator sat. He came from his home in the far North. Wolf was the keeper of the winter. Wolf offered to take the Special Gifts to the farthest North spot. He could bury them in the huge sheet of ice and it would never melt. "They will never want to go there," he said.

Creator pondered Wolf's offer for a while, and then, sadly, shook his head again.

"I think those Two-leggeds will have a curiosity that will make them do things just because they can," he said to Wolf. "They will not ask themselves if they *should,* because they will be so proud of their skills. I think they will make boats that will go *under* the Great Ice, and they will find the Special Gifts."

Creator sat until dawn, thinking. Just before the sun rose again, Earthworm pushed his slippery little nose from the ground, between Creator's feet. Earthworm was startled at first, but then greeted Creator, and asked him what was troubling him. Creator explained the problem.

Earthworm was quiet for a while, and then spoke to Creator.

"I know I am just a small worm, and you are the great Creator. I know you have asked the wisest animals from the farthest places to help you and they could not. I can only dig a small circle here under your feet. I only know about the insides of the Earth, the insides of things, but I have an idea."

"Why don't you take the Special Gifts of Love and Honor and bury them deep inside the *hearts* of the Two-leggeds. They will have to look very hard to find them."

It was a great idea, and that's what Creator did. Creator smiled, and thanked Earthworm for showing that even a humble Earthworm is very important, and can be very wise.

A nd you know, to this day, the only Two-leggeds who have found the Special Gifts are the ones who know where to look.

When someone finds Love and Honor in their heart, the Special Gifts are safe. Forever.

For MaryJo

Author's Note:
This story is adapted from a Lakota year-round tale. My thanks to their original wisdom.

Book design by Russell S. Kuepper

NorthWord Press
5900 Green Oak Drive
Minnetonka, MN 55343
1-800-328-3895

Library of Congress Cataloging-in-Publication Data

Olson, Dennis L.
    Special gifts / by Dennis L. Olson ; illustrations by John F. McGee.
        p.   cm.
        Summary: Afraid that the "Two-leggeds" might use unwisely the special gifts of love and honor, the Creator asks the animals how to protect them.
        ISBN 1-55971-679-7 (hardcover)
        [1. Animals--Fiction. 2. God--Fiction.]   I. McGee, John F., ill.
    II. Title.
    PZ7.051795Sp   1999
    [Fic]--dc21   98-49215

Printed in Malaysia